For Joshua, who loves riding, and for Billy, my own roan rider—M.K.

by Monica Kulling • illustrated by Betina Ogden

A Random House PICTUREBACK® Shape Book

Random House 🏠 New York

Text copyright © 2001 by Random House, Inc. Illustrations copyright © 2001 by Betina Ogden. All rights reserved under International and Pan-American Copyright Conventions. Published in the United States by Random House, Inc., New York, and simultaneously in Canada by Random House of Canada Limited, Toronto.

Library of Congress Cataloging-in-Publication Data: Kulling, Monica. Horses / by Monica Kulling ; illustrated by Betina Ogden. p. cm. — "A Random House pictureback shape book." ISBN 0-375-81217-2 1. Horses—Juvenile literature. 2. Ponies—Juvenile literature. [1. Horses.] I. Ogden, Betina, ill. II. Title. SF302 .K86 2001 636.1—dc21 00-054297

www.randomhouse.com/kids Printed in the United States of America First Edition October 2001 26 25 24 23 22 21 20 19 18

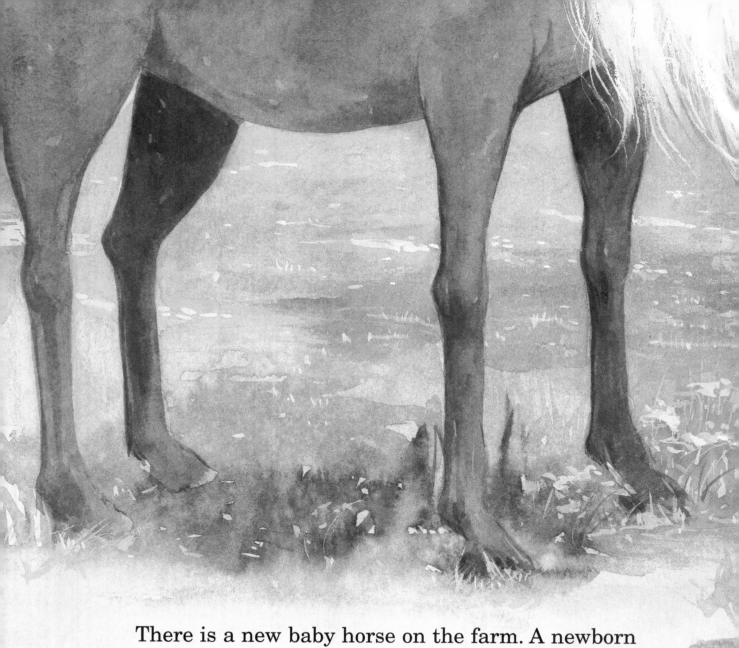

There is a new baby horse on the farm. A newborn horse is called a foal. This foal is male, so he is called a colt. A female foal is called a filly.

As soon as the colt was born, he stood on his wobbly legs. He already weighed 100 pounds!

The colt is brown, like his mother.

But horses come in many different colors. They can be black, brown, white, gold, or gray.

Some even have spots like this Appaloosa . . .

or patches of color like this pinto.

Horses come in many sizes, too. This Morgan is
big and strong. She can easily pull a loaded wagon.

Ponies are small horses. The Shetland pony is one of the smallest horses in the world. When it is full-grown, it stands only four feet high.

The newborn colt is already that tall!

When the colt is a year old, he is called a yearling.
He will be full-grown when he is five years old. The
yearling eats hay, oats, and grass.

Horses also love sweet
things like apples and carrots.

Horses get muddy and dusty and need grooming. The yearling stands still as a currycomb loosens the dirt and a grooming brush sweeps it away.

At night, horses sleep standing up. The yearling
will lie down when he gets tired of standing.

The yearling is now almost two. When he is ready to
be ridden, he will wear a saddle and a bridle. A bridle is
a harness made of metal and leather. The bridle has a
metal bar, called a bit, that goes in the horse's mouth.
This makes it possible for the rider to guide the horse.

Horses need horseshoes before they can be
ridden. A farrier, or blacksmith, comes to the farm
to shoe the horses.

The metal shoes protect the horse's hooves
from the hard road.

The young horse starts off walking.
"Giddyup!" says the rider.

The horse breaks into a trot. A trot is a fast walk.

Now the horse is racing. That's called a gallop.

Hold on tight!
This horse was born to run.